THE SECRET OF THE HIDDEN SCROLLS

BOOK FIVE
THE SHEPHERD'S STONE

BY M. J. THOMAS

WORTHY®
kids

For Tom and Betty Pruitt.
Thank you for your support.

—M.J.T.

ISBN: 978-0-8249-5691-2

WorthyKids
Hachette Book Group
1290 Avenue of the Americas
New York, NY 10104

Library of Congress Cataloging-in-Publication Data
Names: Thomas, M. J., 1969- author
Title: The shepherd's stone / by M. J. Thomas.
Description: Nashville, Tennessee : WorthyKids/ideals, 2018. | Series: Secret
    of the hidden scrolls ; book 5 | Summary: "The mysterious scroll
    transports the time-traveling trio back to Bethlehem where they quickly
    befriend a young David before he faces Goliath"— Provided by publisher.
Identifiers: LCCN 2018040704 | ISBN 9780824956912 (paperback)
Subjects: | CYAC: Time travel—Fiction. | David, King of Israel—Fiction. |
    Jews—History—To 1200 B.C.—Fiction. | Brothers and sisters—Fiction. |
    Dogs—Fiction. | Palestine—History—To 70 A.D.—Fiction. | BISAC:
    JUVENILE FICTION / Religious / Christian / Action & Adventure. | JUVENILE
    FICTION / Readers / Chapter Books.
Classification: LCC PZ7.1.T4654 She 2018 | DDC [Fic]—dc23 LC record available
at https://lccn.loc.gov/2018040704

Cover illustration by Graham Howells
Interior illustrations by Lisa S. Reed and Jerry Pittenger
Designed by Georgina Chidlow-Irvin

Lexile® level 420L

Printed and bound in the U.S.A.
LSC-C
Printing 5, 2021

CONTENTS

PROLOGUE

Nine-year-old Peter and his ten-year-old sister, Mary, stood at the door to the huge, old house and waved as their parents drove away. Peter and Mary and their dog, Hank, would be spending the month with Great-Uncle Solomon.

Peter thought it would be the most boring month ever—until he realized Great-Uncle Solomon was an archaeologist. Great-Uncle Solomon showed them artifacts and treasures and told them stories about his travels around the globe. And then he shared his most amazing discovery of all—the Legend of the Hidden Scrolls! These weren't just dusty old scrolls. They held secrets—and they would lead to travel through time.

Soon Peter, Mary, and Hank were flung back in time to important moments in the Bible. They witnessed the Creation of the earth. They helped Noah load the animals before the flood. They endured the plagues in Egypt. They stood on top of the walls of Jericho as they crumbled to the ground. They had exciting adventures, all while trying to solve the secrets in the scrolls.

Now Peter and Mary are ready for their next adventure . . . as soon as they hear the lion's roar.

The Legend of the Hidden Scrolls

THE SCROLLS CONTAIN THE TRUTH YOU SEEK.
BREAK THE SEAL. UNROLL THE SCROLL.
AND YOU WILL SEE THE PAST UNFOLD.
AMAZING ADVENTURES ARE IN STORE
FOR THOSE WHO FOLLOW THE LION'S ROAR!

THE WOODS

Peter wiggled on the uncomfortable couch covered with flowery pillows in Great-Uncle Solomon's living room. His dog, Hank, was snoring beside him. Hank could sleep anywhere.

Peter looked across the room at Mary. She sat in the big, comfy leather chair reading a book—of course. He tapped his foot louder and louder on the wood floor. He couldn't take it anymore. "This is so boring!" he blurted out.

Mary glanced up from her book for a moment. Then she looked back down.

"It's been two days since our last adventure," groaned Peter. "I'm tired of sitting around."

"You know what the Legend of the Scrolls says," Mary said. "We have to wait for the lion's roar."

"I'm tired of waiting. I'm going to find something to do." Peter hopped off the couch and walked across the room, past the stacks of books, to the tall, wooden front door. He pulled the door open wide.

Peter stepped outside and took a deep breath. He looked out at the woods on the far edge of Great-Uncle Solomon's yard. He stuck his head back inside.

"Hey, Mary!" he said. "Let's go explore the woods."

Hank jumped down and ran outside. He was always up for an adventure.

Mary didn't look up. "Not right now," she said. "I'm reading."

Peter stepped back inside. "What are you reading?"

Mary sighed and held the book up so he could see.

He slowly read the title on the brown, dusty cover, *"Exploring the Great Outdoors."*

She put the book back in her lap and went back to reading.

Peter turned to the woods waiting to be explored. Then he looked back at Mary. He shook his head. "Fine, Hank and I will explore by ourselves."

Mary didn't respond. Peter closed the door and headed across the yard with Hank trailing behind.

The trees seemed to grow taller and taller as Peter and Hank got closer to the woods. Dark clouds started to roll across the sky. The wind howled and the trees creaked.

"Don't worry." Peter glanced at Hank. "There's nothing to be afraid of."

As they entered the woods, the wind blew harder and shadows crept across the moss-covered ground. Peter heard a branch snap ahead of them. He and Hank froze. Peter's heart was thumping so loudly, he could hear it.

Peter squinted as he tried to look through the trees. He didn't see anything moving.

"I think we're okay," said Peter. Then he heard another branch break.

Hank's ears perked up and he barked.

"Maybe we should go back to the house," said Peter, "and wait for Mary to come with us." He turned and ran out of the woods with Hank on his heels.

"*Ruff!*"

Peter stopped. "What are you barking at? Oh! You found your ball! We can play inside while Mary finishes her book."

"That was quick," said Mary, as Peter walked through the door.

"We decided to wait for you," said Peter. "I didn't want you to miss the fun."

"I'm almost finished," said Mary.

Peter tossed the ball over Mary's head. She didn't even look up. Hank ran and brought it back. Peter threw it again.

Crash! Clang!

Mary jumped out of the chair and dropped

her book. "Peter! What did you do?"

Peter ran across the room to the tall, shiny suit of armor. "Oh, no," he said. "We have a little problem." He looked down at the sword lying on the floor. He picked it up and tried to put it back in the knight's iron glove, but the sword wouldn't stay.

Peter felt Mary's eyes on him. He turned to see her standing with her hands on her hips.

"Let me try," she said.

He handed the sword to Mary and stepped back to give her room.

Mary tried to fit the sword back into the glove. She struggled to get the fingers of the armor to hold the sword. "That should do it," she said, backing away from the armor.

Clank! The sword *and* glove fell to the floor.

"Look," said Peter. He pulled a long, rolled-up piece of paper out of the wrist of the armor.

Hank sniffed the paper and barked.

"Put it back," said Mary. "Before Great-Uncle Solomon finds us."

"Are you kidding me?" said Peter. "Maybe it's a clue about our next adventure." Peter knew that Mary loved clues and mysteries.

Mary twisted her hair and looked around the room. "Well, maybe you're right."

Hank wagged his tail.

"Okay," said Mary. "Let's see what it says."

THE ROYAL ROOM

Peter plopped down on the floor in front of the suit of armor. He unrolled the paper and held it flat. "It looks like a map of Great-Uncle Solomon's house."

Mary sat down beside him. "It's a blueprint."

He pointed at a red arrow with the words "You Are Here" written beside it. "I wonder what this means?"

Mary looked at the blueprint, then looked around the room. "The arrow is pointing to the exact spot where we are sitting."

A chill ran through Peter's body. "How does it know?"

Mary shrugged.

Peter studied the rest of the blueprint. There were lots of hallways and rooms.

Mary pointed. "Here's my room, and your room, and the library."

Peter's stomach growled. "There's the kitchen."

Mary ran her finger along a hall of rooms on the other side of the kitchen. "We haven't been to any of these."

"I didn't even know there were rooms over there," said Peter.

"Why is this one circled in red?" said Peter, pointing.

Mary leaned closer. "It says 'The Royal Room.'"

Peter jumped up. "Let's check it out!"

Mary rolled up the blueprint, and they headed to the kitchen.

As Peter walked through the kitchen, he sniffed the air. "Yum. Muffins," he said as he picked up a blueberry muffin off the kitchen counter and took a big bite.

"*Ruff.*" Hank wagged his tail and waited for a treat.

Peter pinched off a small bite and tossed it to Hank. Hank jumped in the air and caught it.

"Come on. Let's find The Royal Room," said Mary. She unrolled the blueprint and spread it out on the table. "We came in through this door." She looked up. "So, The Royal Room must be through that door." She pointed to the door beside the refrigerator.

"I thought that was a pantry," said Peter. He took the last bite of the muffin and opened the door. "Definitely not a pantry!"

The door led to a long hallway with four doors on either side.

"Which one?" asked Peter.

Mary looked at the blueprint again. "The Royal Room is the second door on the right."

Hank ran up and down the hallway sniffing at each door. He stopped at the second door on the right and barked.

"You found it!" said Peter. "You *are* the world's smartest dog." He opened the door and peeked inside.

A throne sat on the far side of the room. Paintings of kings and queens hung on the walls. He walked over to a shelf that held a row of crowns. "Look at these!" Some were big and some were small. Some were covered in jewels and some had no jewels at all.

Peter picked up a small crown in the middle of the shelf and put it on his head. He walked across the room and climbed onto the throne. "I'm the king of the world!"

Mary rolled her eyes and picked up a golden goblet.

"It looks good on you," said Great-Uncle Solomon from the doorway.

Peter gulped. "Thanks. It fits perfectly."

Mary quickly put the goblet back. "The king must have been pretty small," she said.

"God doesn't look on the outside," said Great-Uncle Solomon. "God looks at the heart."

"Who did the crown belong to?" asked Mary.

Great-Uncle Solomon took a closer look at the crown on Peter's head. "It belonged to King Joash," he said. "He became the king of Israel when he was only seven years old."

Peter adjusted the crown. "So, I could be king!"

Great-Uncle Solomon laughed. "Yes, you're old enough to be king."

"I didn't know Israel had kings," said Peter.

"They didn't for a long time," said Great-Uncle Solomon. "God was their king."

"What happened?" asked Mary.

"The Israelites didn't want to listen to God," said Great-Uncle Solomon. "They wanted to have a king like all the other nations." He walked over to the row of crowns. "So, God let them have a king."

Pling! Plunk!

Peter looked down beside the throne and saw Hank strumming strings with his paw.

"Is that some kind of old guitar?" asked Peter.

Mary picked up the dusty, wooden instrument. "No, it's an ancient harp."

Peter sat back in the throne, folded his arms, and waited for a history lesson.

"Harps are one of the oldest musical instruments," she said. "They were played in Egypt more than five thousand years ago."

Great-Uncle Solomon rubbed his chin like he was impressed. "How do you know so much about harps?"

"I read a book," she said. *Be Still My Harp: The History of Stringed Instruments.*

"Whose harp was it?" asked Peter.

"I discovered it on an archaeological dig in an ancient palace in Jerusalem," said Great-Uncle Solomon. "I think it belonged to King—"

Roar!

The lion's roar echoed loudly through the

house. It was so loud it made the crown on Peter's head shake.

"I'll have to tell you later," said Great-Uncle Solomon. "It's time for your next adventure!"

"Let's go!" said Peter.

Peter, Mary, and Hank ran down the hallway and through the kitchen.

"Wait!" Peter said and slid to a stop. He grabbed a few more muffins. "Now we can go."

They ran past the suit of armor and stopped at the library door. Peter reached for the handle shaped like a lion's head.

"Wait!" said Mary. "You forgot to get the adventure bag."

Peter darted through the hallway and grabbed it out of his bedroom. He shoved the muffins in the bag and headed back to the library.

Click. Peter turned the handle and opened the door.

Roar! The sound came from behind the tall bookshelf on the right.

Hank ran to the bookshelf and barked.

Mary pulled a book from the shelf. It was a red book with a lion's head painted in gold on the cover.

The bookshelf rumbled and slid open to reveal a hidden room. It was dark except for a glowing clay pot filled with ancient scrolls in the center of the room.

Peter ran to the pot with Mary and Hank close behind. He shuffled through the scrolls and pulled one out.

"What's on the red wax seal?" asked Mary.

"I think it's a crown," he said.

"Let's see where it takes us," said Mary.

Peter broke the seal. Suddenly, the walls shook, books flew off the shelves, and the floor quaked.

Peter grabbed Mary's hand. "Here we go!"

The library crumbled around them, then everything was still and quiet.

WOLVES!

Peter looked down at the thick, green grass under his feet. Then he looked up at Mary.

She was staring at the top of his head. "You're still wearing the crown," she said. "Hide it before someone sees it!"

Peter put the crown and the scroll in the adventure bag. He was careful not to smash the muffins. He looked around at trees surrounding the green hilltop. "Where are we?"

"I don't know, but we're not in the desert this time," said Mary.

"At least it's not so hot," said Peter.

Hank barked and took off running straight at a flock of fluffy, white sheep eating grass. They ran off in all directions. He barked and ran in a big circle around them. After a couple of minutes, he brought the sheep back together in the center of the grassy hilltop.

"Good boy!" said Peter.

The sheep started munching grass again.

Peter heard a howl coming from the distance.

The sheep lifted their heads, still chewing.

Peter heard another howl, and another. He ran to the crest of the hill and looked down into the valley to investigate. He saw three wolves creeping through bushes and climbing the hill. He turned and ran toward Mary, who was petting one of the wooly lambs.

"Wolves!" shouted Peter. "We need to get out of here!"

The lamb ran away from Mary. Mary's eyes widened in surprise. She looked around. "Let's climb a tree!" she said. "They can't get us up there."

"Are you sure?"

"Yes," said Mary. "I read it in a book called—"

Peter interrupted. "Okay, I believe you!"

Peter and Mary ran to the tallest tree they could find. Peter gave Mary a boost. She climbed the tree like a monkey. He was impressed.

Peter slowly struggled up the tree.

"Hurry!" shouted Mary as she climbed from limb to limb.

"It's hard to climb with the adventure bag," he grunted. "It keeps getting caught on the branches."

Halfway up the tree, Peter looked down at the sheep in the distance. He thought they looked like cotton balls. As he climbed higher, he could also see the wolves creeping closer. Peter started to feel a little dizzy. Peter had never climbed a tree this high before. "I think we're high enough," he said.

He held the adventure bag under one hand and clutched a tree branch with the other. His heart raced. Peter was a little afraid of heights, but he didn't want to admit it to Mary.

He watched the wolf pack crawl closer to the sheep. Then the wolves ran straight for the sheep and Hank.

"Run, Hank!" shouted Peter. "There are too many!"

But Hank didn't run. He stood his ground between the sheep and the wolves. Hank growled. The three wolves snarled and showed their fangs. They circled Hank slowly.

Peter started climbing down the tree to help. The ground seemed so far away, and he felt the tree swaying. His heart pounded. He took short, quick breaths.

"Are you okay?" asked Mary.

Peter hugged the tree trunk and didn't move. "I'm fine," he said. "I just hope Hank is okay."

He wanted to help Hank—but he was afraid to move. The only thing he could do was watch.

Yelp!

One of the wolves shook and ran off.

Yelp! Another wolf was hit by something and ran away.

"Grrrr!" Hank growled at the last wolf.

Peter wondered what was hitting the wolves to scare them off. He looked across the field and saw someone running straight toward Hank and the wolf. The figure looked like a teenage boy. He was wearing a brown robe and sandals and he was shouting and spinning a sling above his head as he ran.

The boy slung a rock through the air. It flew into the side of the last wolf, who yelped and ran away.

Peter let out a breath. "That was close."

"Who is that?" said Mary.

"I don't know," said Peter. "Let's find out."

THE BIG PROBLEM

The boy ran to Hank. "You are very brave," he said. "Thanks for protecting my sheep."

Peter watched Mary quickly climb down past him. He wondered how she was not afraid to fall. He climbed down carefully one branch at a time.

Mary dropped from the lowest limb to the ground. "Thanks for rescuing us!" she shouted.

The young shepherd looked surprised. "I didn't see you over there," he said. "I don't get many visitors while I'm taking care of the sheep."

The shepherd walked over to meet Mary. Hank wagged his tail and followed.

Peter finally made it down to the last branch and dangled above the ground. "Can I get a little help?"

"Here, I'll catch you," said the shepherd. Peter slowly let go of the branch. He was glad to be safe on the ground again.

"My name is David," said the shepherd. He looked Peter up and down. "You don't look like you're from around here."

"I'm Peter, and this is my sister Mary."

"*Ruff!*" Hank sat beside Peter.

"And this is our dog, Hank," said Peter.

"Where did you find this amazing dog?" asked David. "I could use a dog like him to help with the sheep."

"He's an Australian Shepherd," said Peter.

David looked confused. "What's Australian?"

he said. "I don't think I've ever heard of it."

Mary started to explain, but Peter wasn't interested in a geography lesson. He wanted to know more about the sling David was holding.

"How did you do that?" asked Peter.

"God helps me," answered David. "And I have a lot of time to practice while I'm watching the sheep."

"Can you teach me?" said Peter.

"Yes," said David. He looked around the ground and picked up a small rock. He placed the rock in a small pouch in the middle of the sling. "First, you have to spin the sling really fast."

Peter watched David spinning the sling by his side.

"Then you let it fly!" He let go of one end of the sling and sent the rock soaring through the air.

Hank took off like a lightning bolt and brought the rock back.

"Can I try?" asked Peter.

David dug his hand into the small bag hanging by his side. "I think I have an extra sling," he said. "Here it is." He pulled it out and handed it to Peter.

Hank gave the rock to Peter. He put it in the sling and spun it around—faster and faster.

"Now let it fly!" said David.

Peter let it go, and the rock landed about two feet in front of him.

Mary laughed.

Peter ignored her and picked up the rock to

try again. This time the rock flew across the field.

"You're getting the hang of it," said David. "Just keep practicing."

Hank fetched the rock and brought it back to Peter.

"Mary, do you want to try?" asked David.

"No, thanks," said Mary. "I'll stick with karate."

"What's karate?" asked David.

Mary ran and jumped and did a spinning kick in the air.

David clapped his hands. "You'll have to teach me to do that!"

Mary showed David some karate moves while Peter practiced using his sling. Hank kept watch over the sheep.

"I'm hungry," said Peter.

"Me too," said David. "But I didn't bring any food."

"I have some," said Peter. He put his sling in the adventure bag and reached deep into the bag to get the muffins. As he was pulling them out, the crown fell out and rolled across the ground.

Mary gasped.

David picked it up and handed it to Peter. "Are you a king?"

"No," said Peter. "It belongs to my Great-Uncle Solomon."

"Solomon," repeated David. "I like that name. Is Solomon a king?" asked David.

"No," said Mary. "He found the crown."

"So, is he a treasure hunter?" asked David.

"Sort of," said Peter. He didn't say anything else. He didn't want to give away too much.

"Well, I'm going to be king someday," said David.

They sat down to eat the muffins, and David told them how a priest named Samuel had visited his family and told him he was going to be the king of Israel. He was just waiting for the day to come.

David lowered his head and said, "But now I'm afraid that I won't ever be king."

"Why?" asked Peter.

"The kingdom of Israel is facing a big problem," said David. "The Philistines!"

THE LOST SHEEP

"Who are they?" asked Peter.

"The Philistines are our enemy," said David. "They have a huge army, and they want to destroy the kingdom of Israel."

"That doesn't sound good," said Peter.

David shook his head. "If they destroy us, I will never be king."

"Isn't there anything you can do?" asked Mary.

"I wish there was," said David. "Three of my older brothers have been away at the battle for forty days, but I'm stuck here watching the sheep."

"What's it like being a shepherd?" she asked.

"I spend most of my time reading and writing poetry and songs," said David.

Mary leaned in closer. "What do you read?"

"I read scrolls about the history of our people," said David.

"That sounds boring," muttered Peter.

"But sometimes it's exciting and dangerous being a shepherd!" said David.

Now Peter was interested.

"I love my sheep," said David. "I would do anything to protect them."

"How many do you have?" asked Mary.

"I have exactly one hundred sheep," said David. He looked around. "That reminds me— I need to count to make sure they all came back after the wolf scare."

David stood up and looked around the pasture. It took a while to count because he had a lot of sheep. "Ninety-seven, ninety-eight, ninety-nine . . ." He spun around with a look of panic. "One of my sheep is missing!" said David. "We have to find it!"

"What can we do to help?" said Mary.

"I have to leave the rest of the sheep here," said David. "Mary, can you and Hank stay and watch over them?" Then he looked at Peter. "Can you help me search?"

Peter left the adventure bag with Mary. "Let's find that sheep!"

David picked up his shepherd's staff, and they were off. They searched all through the trees at the edge of the pasture.

"Pearl!" shouted David. "Where are you?"

"Your sheep have names?" asked Peter.

"Yes," said David. "I name all of them."

Peter looked around.

"What does Pearl look like?"

"She's a fluffy, white lamb," said David.

"That doesn't help much," said Peter.

"I'll know her," said David. "The wolves
must have scared her."

David and Peter couldn't find Pearl in the
woods. They couldn't find Pearl by the stream.
Peter felt like they had been searching for hours.
The sun began to set behind the hills.

"There's one more place she could be," said David.

Peter followed David up a steep hill. They climbed higher and higher until they reached the tip-top.

"Pearl!" David's voice echoed in the surrounding hills.

Baaaa!

Peter heard the lamb's cry from the other side of the steep bluff.

David dropped his staff and ran to the edge. He looked down. "Oh, Pearl, what have you gotten yourself into?"

Peter stayed back at a safe distance. "Do you see her?"

"Yes," said David. "Come here and take a look."

Peter carefully walked to the edge and stared down the cliff. It dropped straight down. Sharp rocks and a few thorny branches poked from the side of the cliff. It was so high that Peter couldn't see the bottom through the growing darkness.

Then he saw the little lamb stuck on one of the branches about ten feet down. Peter's heart pounded, and his stomach started feeling queasy. He slowly backed away from the edge.

"Are you okay?" asked David. "You look like you're about to throw up."

Peter took a few more steps back and took a deep breath. "I'm fine."

Baaaa!

"If you're okay," said David, "I'm going to get Pearl."

"Good idea," said Peter, trying to sound okay. "I'll wait right here."

David walked to the edge of the cliff and disappeared over the side. Peter heard David slip and gravel bouncing down the side of the cliff.

"Are you okay?" shouted Peter.

"Yes!" answered David. "But I need your help!"

"What do you need?" asked Peter. He didn't want to look.

"I need you to bring me my staff," said David.

Peter found the staff and crawled on his hands and knees to the edge of the cliff. He peeked over. David was about five feet down and dangling from a sharp rock by his fingertips.

David looked into Peter's eyes. "Reach down with the staff," he grunted. "I can't hold on much longer."

Peter gripped the staff in his hand—but he couldn't move. He was frozen with fear.

A Brave Rescue

Peter backed away from the edge of the cliff. "I can't," he said. I'm afraid of heights."

"Me too," said David.

Peter scooted back toward the edge. "You don't look like you're afraid."

David struggled and dug his fingers into the edge of the rock. "I trust God," grunted David. "He will help me."

Peter took another deep breath and inched closer to the edge. Some gravel fell down the cliff.

Peter moaned.

"Trust God!" said David. "He will help you too."

"I do," said Peter. "But that's a long way to fall."

"God made these mountains," said David. "You can trust him. He is bigger than the mountains."

Peter closed his eyes and held the staff over the edge.

"I can almost reach it!" said David. "Just a little bit more."

Peter tried to move closer. "I can't!"

"Pray," said David. "God will free you from your fears."

Peter said, "God, give me strength and help me to help David." He took a deep breath, slid closer to the edge, and reached the staff farther down. He felt David grab the end of the staff.

"Got it!" shouted David. "Now hold tight."

Peter gripped the staff with both hands. He finally opened his eyes and watched as David pulled himself up on top of a rock poking out of the side of the cliff.

"You did it!" said David. "You can let go."

Peter released his grip.

Baaaa!

David reached down from the rock ledge with the staff and hooked it around the lamb.

He pulled her out of the thorny branch into the safety of his arms.

"Back up a little bit," David said.

Peter scooted back and saw the staff hook onto the ledge. Then David's head poked over the top, and he set the lamb beside Peter.

Baaaa! Peter picked up the little lamb and held her in his arms.

David crawled over the ledge. "Now, let's get back to the rest of the sheep."

Peter carried the lamb down the hill, over the stream, and through the woods. It was a little harder in the darkness, but they finally made it back.

"Ruff!" Hank came running across the grassy pasture. He was so excited that he knocked over Peter and the lamb. He licked Peter.

Mary ran up. "What took so long?" she said. "I was so worried."

Peter wiped Hank's slobber off his face. "Look who we found."

Baaaa! The little lamb hopped through the grass and ran to her mom.

"It's getting late," said David. "You two can sleep in my tent, but I need to go and get something first." David walked over to his tent in the trees and brought back a small harp.

A chill ran through Peter's body. "That looks just like—"

Mary elbowed Peter in his ribs and gave him the look.

"Looks just like what?" asked David.

"It looks just like a harp," answered Mary, glaring at Peter.

"Do you play?" asked David.

"No," said Mary. "But I wish I could."

"I can teach you," said David. "First, I need to play so the sheep will go to sleep."

David played the harp and sang. Everyone enjoyed the music—even the sheep. One by one, the sheep closed their eyes.

David handed the harp to Mary and taught her to play a few notes. He stood up and let out a big yawn. "Just keep practicing," said David.

David settled under a tree, and Hank slept beside the sheep. Mary and Peter headed to the tent. It was small, but it was big enough for both of them.

Mary sat in the tent and softly practiced playing the harp.

Peter heard a noise outside of the tent. "Shhhh!"

Mary stopped playing and sat completely still.

"David, is that you?" whispered Peter.

The tent flap slowly opened. It wasn't David—it was Michael the angel.

"Where have you been?" said Mary. "We've

had a lot of problems!"

The adventure bag shook, and Peter pulled out the scroll.

"Don't open it yet," said Michael. "Let me go over the rules of your adventure."

Michael held up one finger. "First rule: you have to solve the secret of the scroll in four days, or you will be stuck here."

Mary gasped. "We only have *four* days? How can we solve it in only *four* days?"

"I don't make the rules," said Michael.

Mary started biting her nails. "We'll never get back to see our parents."

Peter looked at Mary and frowned. They usually had longer to solve the secret message. He started to open the scroll so they could get started solving the scroll.

"Not yet," said Michael. "I need to finish the rules."

Michael held up two fingers. "Second rule: you can't tell anyone where you are from or that you came from the future."

Peter and Mary nodded their heads.

Michael held up three fingers. "Third rule: you can't try to change the past. Okay, now you can open the scroll."

Peter quickly unrolled it. "It's eight words written in Hebrew."

"*Eight* words?" Mary said. "We have less time and more words?"

Peter put his hand on Mary's arm. "We can do it, Mary. You're good at solving problems."

The last word on the scroll glowed and transformed into the word PROBLEMS.

Peter grinned. "One down!"

Mary studied the scroll and pointed. "Hey, isn't that the Hebrew word for God?

The scroll shook, and the third word glowed and transformed into the word GOD. It said:

_____ _____. GOD

_____ _____ _____

_____ PROBLEMS.

"You're off to a good start," said Michael. "Just remember to be on guard for the enemy—Satan. He wants to destroy the

Israelites, and he doesn't want David to become king."

Michael spread his mighty wings. "Now get some sleep. You have a big journey ahead of you." Then he flew into the starry sky.

Meeting The Family

Baaaa! Baaaa!

Peter sat up and yawned. He looked out of the tent where the sun was rising over the hills. "Those sheep sure do wake up early." He crawled out of the tent and stretched.

"Rise and shine and give God the glory!" sang David, as he walked along the grassy pasture.

Mary poked her head out of the tent.

"Sing with me," said David.

Peter rubbed the sleep out of his eyes. "I'm not exactly a morning person."

"Me either," said Mary, brushing her messy hair out of her eyes.

"Ruff! Ruff!" Hank ran up to David and barked and wagged his tail.

"It looks like Hank is ready to go," said Peter.

"A shepherd's day starts early," said David.

Peter heard a horn blast in the distance. "What's that?"

"That's my dad's shofar," said David. "Let's go see what he wants."

"Where's your house?" asked Mary.

"Follow me," said David.

Peter grabbed the adventure bag out of the tent. "I'm ready."

Peter, Mary, and the sheep followed behind David. Peter turned and saw Hank behind the line of sheep, making sure they didn't get lost.

The group walked through the trees to the ridge on the side of a hill. Peter looked into the

valley and saw
a little town filled
with small houses made of stones.

David stretched out his arm. "Welcome to Bethlehem," he said.

Peter hummed the tune of "O Little Town of Bethlehem" as they walked down the hillside.

They found David's father waiting outside the front of the house with a large basket of food at his feet. He glanced at Peter and Mary, but he didn't say anything.

"Good morning," said David. "Did you call for me?"

"Yes," said his father. "Take this basket of roasted grain and loaves of bread to your brothers on the battlefield."

Peter's stomach growled.

"Don't forget the cheese!" came a woman's voice from inside the house. She walked out wearing a long white robe and carrying ten chunks of cheese.

"Good morning, mother," said David.

She gave him a big hug. "How's my baby boy?"

David's cheeks turned red. "I'm fine."

"You didn't tell me we had company," she said. "Introduce me to your guests."

"This is Peter and this is Mary," said David. "They're from Australian."

"Oh, you mean Australia—we're not from there," said Mary. "Our dog is."

Hank barked and wagged his tail.

"Well, that's wonderful," said David's mom. "You all look hungry."

Peter nodded with a grin.

"Please come in and have some cheese," she said. "It's the best cheese in Bethlehem."

"They don't have time," said David's dad. "They need to take the food to the battlefield."

David's mom waved her hand in the air. "There's always time to eat," she said. "And they have a long journey ahead."

Peter rubbed his belly. "I would love some cheese."

"Come in, come in," said David's mom.

Peter followed her into the stone house. He saw three boys sitting on pillows on the floor eating bread and cheese.

"These are three of my brothers: Ozem, Nethaneel, and Raddai," said David.

"Well, well, look who's here," said Ozem. He held his nose. "What's that smell?"

The other brothers laughed.

"Yuck," said Ozem. "It smells like dirty sheep."

"Be nice to your baby brother," said David's mom. "He's going to be king someday."

"Yeah, right," said Ozem. "That little, stinky shepherd will never be king."

The brothers laughed.

"Yes, he will," said Peter. As soon as the words came out of his mouth, Peter knew he shouldn't have said them.

Mary glared at Peter.

"That old priest was crazy," said Ozem. "He should have anointed me king."

David's mother put her arm around David's shoulders. "Remember, God doesn't look on the outside—he looks at the heart."

David's brothers rolled their eyes. "We're

leaving," said Ozem. "It stinks in here." He bumped into David as he walked past.

"I see why you spend so much time in the fields," muttered Peter.

"Sit, sit," said David's mother.

David, Peter, and Mary sat on the pillows.

"Zeruiah and Abigail!" shouted David's mom. "Please come here!"

Two girls came in from the next room.

The oldest ran over and hugged David. "You're home," said Zeruiah. "It's so good to see you."

"Who are your friends?" asked Abigail.

"They're from Australia," said David's mom.

"We're not from Australia," said Peter.

"Well, wherever you're from," she said. "You're welcome here."

Peter's stomach rumbled. "May I have some cheese, please?"

"Of course you can," she said.

David's mother and sisters left the room and came back with blocks of cheese and loaves of bread.

Peter took a big bite of cheese.

Mary elbowed Peter in the ribs. "Thank you," she said.

"Oh, yeah," said Peter with a mouth full of cheese. "Thanks, it's delicious."

"Ruff!" Hank wagged his tail.

They ate until they couldn't eat anymore.

Soon David's father stuck his head in the door. "You need to get going," he said. "It's going to be dark before you get to the battlefield."

Peter stuffed some bread and cheese into his bag for later.

"Don't forget to give the cheese to the captain," said David's dad. "And bring back a report on how your older brothers are doing."

"I will," said David. He picked up the basket of food, and they headed out.

"Who will take care of the sheep while we go to the battlefield?" asked Mary.

"I thought you and Hank could," said David. "You did such a good job yesterday."

"What about Peter?" said Mary.

"He can come with me," said David.

"Why can't I go?" said Mary.

"Because you're a girl," said David, "and girls aren't allowed on the battlefield."

Peter wasn't sure about this. He wanted to go with David, but he didn't want to leave Mary behind.

THE DARK VALLEY OF DEATH

Mary stood up straight. "That's not fair," she said.

"I didn't make the rules," said David.

"Girls are strong too," said Mary.

Peter nodded his head in agreement and said, "She's pretty tough."

"She may be tough," said David, "but girls aren't allowed."

Mary scratched her head. "I have an idea!"

"What?" said David.

"Do you have any old clothes?" asked Mary.

"Sure," said David, "back at the house."

"Don't go anywhere," said Mary. "I'll be right back!" She turned and ran to the house.

"What is she up to?" said David.

"I have no idea," said Peter. "I never know what she's thinking."

Peter, David, and Hank waited and waited. A boy wearing a long robe and a headscarf started walking toward them with something in his hands.

"Excuse me," said David. "Have you seen a girl wearing strange clothes?"

The boy didn't say anything but kept walking closer. Hank barked. Then he ran up and sniffed the boy and started wagging his tail.

Peter squinted his eyes and laughed. "That's not a boy," he said. "That's Mary."

Mary spun around. "How do you like my disguise? Do I look like a boy?"

David laughed. "You fooled me."

"So, can I go to the battlefield?" she said.

David rubbed his chin. "Yes," he said finally. "Let's all go! I have a friend I can ask to watch the sheep."

Mary tossed a robe to Peter. "Put this on so you blend in better."

Peter slipped the robe over his clothes. "Let's go!" said Peter.

As they left Bethlehem, David stopped to talk to his friend. "We're taking food to my brothers," said David. "Can you watch my sheep for a few days?"

"Sure, but be careful," said David's friend. He looked at Peter and Mary. "The battlefield really isn't safe for little boys," he added.

Peter nudged Mary with his elbow. "Your disguise is working," he whispered.

"God will protect us," said David.

They left the sheep and headed toward the battlefield. It was a long journey across hills and rough terrain. They took turns carrying the heavy basket of food.

After walking for what seemed like hours, Peter groaned, "How long until we get there?"

"It's still pretty far," said David.

"My feet are killing me," moaned Mary.

"I know a shortcut," said David. "But it can be dangerous."

Mary stopped and rubbed her feet. "Let's take the shortcut."

"Just a little bit farther," said David.

They approached a narrow valley with tall, rocky cliffs on either side. The sun was beginning to set, and shadows filled the valley.

"*Grrrr!*" Hank growled at the valley.

Peter's heart pounded. "I don't know about this."

"It's called the Dark Valley of Death," said David.

Peter shivered. "I can see why."

"Maybe we should go the long way," said Mary with a quiver in her voice. She stood very still and stared into the shadowy valley. "I don't know if I can do it."

"It will take too long to turn back now," said David.

"But don't be afraid." He reached into his bag and pulled out a scroll. "I wrote a poem that might help." David unrolled the scroll and read:

The Lord is my shepherd.
I have everything I need.
He lets me rest in green pastures.
He leads me beside quiet streams.
He refreshes my soul.
He leads me down the right path
   to show he is good.
Even when I walk through the
   Dark Valley of Death,
I will not fear—because you are with me.
Your rod and staff
   protect and comfort me.

David put the scroll back in his bag.

"I'm not really into poetry," said Peter. "But that was good!"

"God has helped me through the Dark Valley many times," said David. "Don't be afraid—he is with us."

"I believe we can do it!" said Peter.

Mary took a step forward. "I won't let fear stop me."

The bag shook under Peter's arm. He said, "Can Mary and I have a minute? We need to talk about something."

"Sure," said David. "I'll be right over there."

Peter opened his bag and pulled out the shaking scroll.

"Is everything okay over there?" said David. "We need to hurry before it's completely dark!"

"We'll be right there," said Peter.

"Let's see what it says," whispered Mary.

Peter unrolled the scroll. The first word glowed and transformed into the word: FEAR.

Peter read the scroll. "FEAR ___. GOD ____ ____ ____ ____ PROBLEMS."

Mary sighed. "We still have a lot of the secret to solve and not much time."

"God has always been with us," said Peter. "And he has always helped us make it through."

"That's true," said Mary.

They ran over and joined David.

"Is everyone ready?" asked David.

Peter and Mary nodded.

"Woof!" Hank barked and wagged his tail.

"Here we go!" said David. "Stay close together and watch out for bears and lions and snakes."

Peter gulped. "Why are there always snakes?"

As they entered the Dark Valley of Death, Peter looked up at the sides of the cliffs towering above his head. The shadows faded into darkness as the sun set behind the mountains.

"Ouch!" shouted Mary.

Peter turned and saw Mary sitting on the ground holding her ankle.

Hank ran over and licked her ankle.

"Oh, no! Did a snake bite you?" asked Peter.

Mary struggled to her feet. "No, I tripped on a rock."

"We have to keep moving," said David. "It's getting darker."

Mary took a step and grimaced in pain. "I think I'm okay."

"Here, take my staff," said David. "It will help you walk."

Mary took a few steps with the staff. "That's better," she said. "Let's keep going."

They headed deeper into the valley. It got darker and darker. The moonlight at the end of the valley was the only light they could see. Hank walked beside Mary. She was moving a little slower than the rest.

"Grrrrr!"

Peter heard a growl coming from in front of them.

"What was that?" said Mary quietly.

Hank ran in front of them and growled into the darkness.

In the moonlight, Peter saw the silhouette of a tall, shadowy creature standing in front of them.

A Little Close

"Grrrrr!" The creature shuffled forward a few feet.

"Don't move," whispered David. "It's a bear."

The bear sniffed the air and licked its lips.

"Maybe he wants our food," said Mary.

The bear snarled and took another step toward them.

"Maybe he thinks *we're* the food," said Peter.

"Don't move," David said again. "God will help us."

The bear took another step forward. He was close enough that Peter could see his sharp claws.

David slowly set the basket of food on the ground. He reached into his bag and pulled out his sling. Then he picked up a rock. "Let's spread out," said David. "Peter, you go to the left, and I'll go to the right. Mary, don't move."

"But I thought you said to stay together," said Mary.

"Change of plans," said David. He slowly walked to the right side of the bear. He slipped the rock into his sling.

Hank stood guard in front of Mary.

Peter took out his sling and picked up a rock. He walked to the left of the bear, being careful not to make any sudden movements.

David started spinning his sling. "On the count of three," whispered David.

The bear turned toward David. The bear circled his head as he watched the spinning sling.

"One, two . . ." counted David.

Peter put the rock in the sling and started spinning as fast as he could.

The bear got down on all fours and crept toward David.

"Three!" shouted David. He slung the rock through the air. It hit the bear right in the snout.

"Grrrrr!" The bear stood up on his back legs and grabbed his face.

Peter slung his rock and hit the bear in his side. The bear stumbled back across some rocks.

"Good shot!" said David.

"I think you got him!" cheered Mary.

The bear looked up at Mary and snarled through his sharp white fangs.

She hobbled back a few steps. "Or maybe not!"

The bear started to run straight at Mary. Peter couldn't believe how fast he was.

"*Ruff!*" Hank barked fiercely and stood in front of Mary.

"Help!" shouted Mary. She got in a karate pose and held the staff in front of her.

David put another stone in his sling and ran toward the bear. He sent the stone flying through the air. The rock hit the bear and sent him tumbling and rolling across the rocky ground.

The bear slowly stood up and shook his head.

Peter said, "Maybe he's had enough of this fight."

Hank ran closer and barked at the bear. The bear turned and ran out of the Dark Valley, with Hank barking and nipping at his heels.

Peter squinted. He couldn't see Hank or the bear. "Hank!"

Nothing.

"Hank!" shouted Peter again.

Hank came running back to Peter with his tongue hanging out.

"Good boy!" said Peter.

Mary took a deep breath. "That was way too close!"

"We *bearly* made it," said Peter with a grin.

Mary didn't laugh—she never laughed at his jokes.

"We make a good team," said David.

"Yes," said Mary, "especially when God is on our team."

The bag shook, and Peter held it tight so David wouldn't notice.

"You're such a good dog," said David. He bent over and started petting Hank. Peter and Mary walked a few feet away and turned their backs toward David and Hank. Peter pulled out the shaking scroll. He unrolled it just enough to see that the fourth word glowed and transformed into the word: IS.

Mary peered over his arm. "FEAR ____. GOD IS ____ ____ ____ PROBLEM."

Peter put the scroll back in the bag. He and Mary walked back to David and Hank.

Peter and Mary followed David through the valley. Hank ran ahead of them. When they finally made it to the other side of the valley, it was too dark and too late to continue.

"We'll sleep here and go to the battlefield in the morning," said David.

"What about the bear?" said Mary.

"He's not coming back," said David. "Trust me on that."

David built a small fire out of twigs and branches they found on the ground. They sat around the fire and warmed themselves in the cool night air.

"Why weren't you afraid of that bear?" asked Mary.

David tossed a twig in the fire. "I was afraid."

"You didn't act like it," said Peter.

"I've learned to overcome my fear," said David.

"How?" asked Peter.

"I trust God," said David. "I pray and I remember."

Mary scooted back and waved the smoke out of her eyes. "Remember what?"

"I remember all the times God has helped me before," said David. "And I remember hearing about all the things he has done in the past."

"Like what?" said Peter.

David rubbed his hands near the fire. "I remember when he rescued me from a lion. I also remember the stories of how God rescued Noah from the flood and parted the Red Sea so that Israel could be set free from Pharaoh."

Peter leaned back and looked up at the stars. "I remember that."

David leaned toward Peter. "What do you mean?"

Mary poked Peter with her elbow. "He means that he remembers reading about it."

"Yeah," said Peter. "Those are great stories."

"They're not just stories," said David. "They're true."

"I believe you," said Peter. "Trust me—I know they're true."

"So, I trust God, and it helps me overcome my fear," said David. "Because God is the same yesterday, today, and forever."

David stood up and kicked sand on the fire. The flames died, and smoke drifted into the sky. "Now let's get some sleep. We have a big day ahead of us."

While David, Mary, and Hank drifted off to sleep, Peter pulled the adventure journal out of his bag. He wrote by the light of the moon.

Day 2

We're on our way to the battlefield. I'm a little nervous, but I know God is with us. I've learned so much from David. He's helped me to trust God and face my fears. This adventure is going so fast. We only have two days left. I hope we can solve the secret of the scroll in time.

Peter put the journal away. He rested his head on the adventure bag and gazed at the stars. He wasn't as afraid anymore.

A Giant Problem

The sun rose over the hills and woke Peter. He stretched and his stomach growled.

"Time for breakfast," Peter called to Mary and David. He pulled out bread and cheese from his bag and shared it with the others.

They ate and talked about the bear and the Dark Valley of Death.

Peter looked back into the sun-filled valley. "It doesn't look so scary anymore," he said, eating his last bite of cheese.

David stood up and grabbed the basket of

food. "It's time for us to go to the battlefield."

Mary wrapped her hair in a bun and tucked it under her headscarf. "Let's go," she said in her deepest boy-sounding voice.

She stood up and took a few steps with David's staff. She didn't limp at all. "I don't think I need this any longer."

The adventure bag shook on the ground. Hank ran over and barked at the bag.

"Is something wrong with your bag?" asked David.

Peter picked the bag up and tried to think of something quickly. "No more cheese for you, Hank," he said. "He just loves cheese."

"My mother does make good cheese," said David.

Mary handed the staff to David. "You go ahead," she said. "I need to talk to Peter for a minute."

"Sure," said David. "Let's go, Hank. They need a little privacy."

Peter pulled the scroll out of the bag and unrolled it. The seventh word on the scroll glowed and transformed into the word: ANY. Peter read, "FEAR ____. GOD IS ____ ____ ANY PROBLEM."

Peter looked at Mary. She frowned. "We still have three words to solve," she said, "by tomorrow."

"We don't have time to solve it now," Peter said. "We need to keep moving!" He put the scroll back in the bag, and they ran to catch up with David and Hank.

It didn't take long to get to the battlefield. Peter saw smoke rising in front of them. They climbed the hill and found the Israelite camp. Small white tents covered the hilltop. One large tent sat in the middle. Two soldiers with shields and long, sharp spears stood guard at the entrance. They didn't move a muscle.

"Someone important must be in there," said Peter.

"That's King Saul's tent," said David. "Let's keep going. We need to find my brothers."

One of the guards gave Peter a suspicious look as he walked past. They looked all around but couldn't find David's brothers. So David left the basket of food with the keeper of the supplies.

"The cheese is for the captain," David said. "The rest is for my brothers—Eliab, Abinadab, and Shammah."

"I'll make sure they get the food," the keeper said. "Be careful out there."

"We will," said Mary in her regular voice.

The man looked at Mary. "What?"

Mary coughed and cleared her throat. "We will," she said in her deepest, gruffest voice.

"Prepare for battle!" came a shout from within the camp.

Soldiers scurried everywhere—grabbing shields and swords and helmets. They shouted and clanged their swords against their shields. Peter could feel the excitement in the air!

The battle horn blasted, and the soldiers lined up near the hillside. They stretched from one end of the steep hill to the other.

"There are my brothers!" said David. He pointed and ran ahead.

Peter, Mary, and Hank followed. David ran to the middle of the line of soldiers. He tapped one of the tallest soldiers on his shoulder.

The soldier turned and gave David a look that Peter recognized. He glanced at Mary. It was the look Mary gave him every time he did or said something wrong.

"What are you doing here?" grunted David's brother.

"I brought food," said David, "from home."

Eliab rolled his eyes and looked at Peter, Mary, and Hank. "Stand back," he said, "the battlefield is no place for little boys—or dogs." Then he turned back to face the valley.

Peter heard the slow, steady beat of drums echoing across the valley. The Israelite soldiers became quiet and stood their ground. The drumbeat grew louder and louder. Peter looked across the valley and saw the Philistine soldiers line up on the hill on the opposite side of the valley. The sun reflected off their swords and shields.

"Halt!" shouted the captain of the Philistine army. The drumming stopped, and the soldiers stood still.

The men in the two armies glared at each other across the valley.

Peter turned to David. "Why aren't they moving? Shouldn't they be fighting?"

"I'm not sure," said David.

Peter squeezed between two soldiers to get a better look. Mary, Hank, and David wiggled past his big brothers and joined him.

Peter looked across the valley. The soldiers in the middle of the Philistine line moved apart, and a giant man stepped between them. The other soldiers only came up to his chest! The giant lifted his huge spear into the air and roared. The Philistine soldiers chanted, "Goliath, Goliath, Goliath!"

Peter looked around. The Israelite soldiers were frozen in frightened silence.

Goliath slowly marched down into the valley. Peter had never seen anybody so tall before. His leather sandals pounded the sandy ground, leaving a trail of dust behind him. He was covered in bronze armor from head to toe. He carried his spear in one hand and a sword on his belt. A soldier wearing black armor from head to toe walked in front of him, carrying a bronze shield with a slithery black snake painted on it.

Goliath stopped in the middle of the valley. "Why are you all coming out to fight?" he shouted. "I am the Philistine champion, but you are only the servant of your tiny, little King Saul." He laughed and the soldiers jeered.

"I have a deal for you!" Goliath said. "Choose one man to come down here and fight me! If he kills me, we will be your slaves. But if I kill him, you will be our slaves!"

Not a single Israelite soldier moved forward to accept Goliath's challenge. In fact, some turned and ran back to the camp.

"The army of Israel is a bunch of cowards!" Goliath shouted. He turned and marched back up the hill.

David clenched his fists. "Why won't anyone fight him?" he shouted to the Israelite soldiers.

"Goliath has been threatening us for many days," said one soldier. "But he is so huge. No one wants to accept his challenge."

David asked another soldier standing nearby, "Who does he think he is to come against the armies of God?"

"Why don't you fight him then?" said another soldier.

"Maybe I will," said David.

Peter looked over at David's brothers. Their faces were red. Peter couldn't tell if they were more embarrassed or mad.

"What are you doing here anyway?" said Eliab. "Go home and take care of your little sheep. Leave the fighting to the men!"

"What have I done now?" said David. "I was only asking a question!"

One of the king's guards walked up behind David.

"*Grrrr!*" Hank growled at the guard.

The guard tapped David on the shoulder.

David spun around and looked up at the tall, serious guard.

"The king wants to see you!" he grunted at David.

"Now you're in trouble," said Eliab.

THE KING

"Why does King Saul want to see me?" asked David.

"I don't know," said the guard. "Follow me!"

David followed the guard. Peter, Mary, and Hank followed close behind. They arrived at the entrance of the big tent.

The guard opened the tent flap. "The king will see you now."

David bowed as he entered. Then Peter and Mary entered and bowed.

The guard put his shield down in front of

Hank. "No animals allowed in the king's tent!"

"*Grrrr!*" Hank growled at the guard.

"It's okay, Hank," said Peter. "Stay here. We'll be right back."

Hank sat down beside the guards and kept watch.

"Whoa," said Peter. "This tent is huge!"

Torches filled the tent with light, and colorful rugs covered the sandy ground. A large wooden table sat in the center of the tent covered in maps and scrolls. Armor and weapons filled one corner. It was the fanciest tent Peter had ever seen.

Peter looked across the tent. King Saul sat on a large golden throne. He wore a colorful robe and a golden crown on his head. His long brown beard had streaks of gray running through it. King Saul stood and walked toward David. Peter was surprised by how tall he was. He wasn't as tall as Goliath, but he was tall.

"It's good to see you, David," the king said.

David pointed at Peter and Mary. "These are my friends. They helped me bring food to my brothers."

"Welcome," said King Saul. He lowered his head and sighed.

"How can I help you, King?" said David. "Do you want me to play the harp for you?"

"Not today," said King Saul. "Your harp won't help me with the problem I am facing."

Peter thought about Goliath. He was definitely a big problem.

"Don't worry about the giant Philistine," said David. "I will fight him!"

King Saul shook his head. "There's no way you can fight Goliath and win!" he said. "You're too young."

David stood tall and brave. "I've been protecting my sheep," he said. "When a lion or a bear comes to steal a lamb, I go after it and rescue the lamb. If the animal turns on me, I defeat it."

Peter stepped forward. "It's true! I saw him defeat a bear."

"And wolves!" said Mary, in her deep voice.

King Saul walked over to the table and moved some scrolls around. "I don't know . . ."

David walked to the other side of the table and looked into King Saul's eyes. "The Lord has rescued me from the claws of lions and bears. He will rescue me from this Philistine who has come against the armies of God!"

King Saul rubbed his beard. Finally, he said, "All right. You will fight Goliath." The king walked over to the armor. "I have some things here that will help you in the battle tomorrow."

David slipped on the clunky bronze vest—it came down to his knees. He put on a bronze helmet—it wobbled on his head and covered his eyes. He strapped a long sword around his waist—it almost touched the ground. David walked stiffly past Peter and Mary.

He peeked out from under the helmet. "I can't wear these," he said to the king. He took off the armor. "God will protect me."

"All right, go ahead," said King Saul. "And may the Lord be with you!"

David walked out of the tent. "Let's go," Peter said to Mary. Hank was waiting outside and joined them.

Word quickly spread through the camp that David was going to face Goliath.

David, Peter, and Mary walked across the camp between the small white tents. Peter heard the soldiers whispering as David walked by. The soldiers shook their heads and went back to tending their fires.

"Woof!" Hank barked and ran behind one of the tents.

Peter and Mary ran to see what Hank was barking at. When they rounded the corner, Peter saw a soldier dressed in black armor running away.

"Stay, Hank," said Peter.

"That looked like the soldier who was carrying Goliath's shield," said Mary.

"What is he doing over here?" asked Peter.

"Maybe he was spying," said Mary.

"We'll have to be on the lookout for him," said Peter.

They ran back around the tent and caught up with David. He walked with purpose, and he didn't stop walking until they made it to the edge of the hill outside the Israelite camp. David looked down into the valley. He leaned on his staff but didn't say a word.

The sun began to set, and shadows stretched across the valley.

Finally, David turned back to Peter and Mary. "Let's get some sleep," he said. "We have a big day tomorrow."

They found a spot at the edge of the camp. Peter lay down and stared up at the starry sky. He heard Mary settle near him, and it wasn't long before David was snoring. Peter was surprised that David could fall asleep so quickly with such a big challenge ahead of him.

Peter sat up and pulled the adventure journal out of his bag and wrote under the moonlight.

Day 3

We have a big day tomorrow. David is going to face Goliath and the future of the kingdom is up to him. I'm learning so much from David about trusting God. We only have one day left to solve the scroll. I don't trust the soldier in black armor. There's something suspicious about him.

"Grrrr." Hank made a low growl. Peter put the journal away and looked in the direction Hank was growling. He saw the soldier dressed in black running out of the Israelite camp and heading for the valley.

Peter shook Mary's shoulder to wake her up.

Mary rubbed her eyes. "What?"

Peter pointed at the soldier just as he was going over the ledge.

"This can't be good," whispered Mary. "What should we do?"

Peter looked over at David. He was still sleeping. "I think we need to go on a spy mission," whispered Peter.

Hank's ears perked up.

Peter grabbed the bag. "Let's go."

THE SOLDIER OF DARKNESS

Peter and Mary tiptoed past David. Hank crawled past on his belly. They hurried to the cliff on the side of the hill and looked down into the valley. Peter saw the soldier in black running across the valley. He jumped over the stream and started up the hill on the other side.

"Let's hurry, before we lose him!" said Mary.

Peter, Mary, and Hank headed down into the valley. They waded across the shallow stream and ran up the side of the hill. They stopped when they made it to the Philistine camp.

Mary panted. "Where did he go?"

Peter looked around at all of the small white tents. "I don't know," he said. "He could be anywhere."

Hank sniffed the air, then took off running between two tents. Peter and Mary followed him. They ducked and dodged through the tents, so they wouldn't be seen. They found Hank beside a large tent on alert.

"Ha, ha, ha!" a thundering laugh came from the tent.

Peter and Mary crept closer to the tent.

"A boy!" shouted a booming voice. "They're sending a boy to fight me?"

"Yes," said another voice. "I heard them talking about it in their camp."

"I recognize that voice," said Mary.

"I think it's Goliath," said Peter.

"No, not him—the other man's voice," said

Mary. "It reminds me of the enemy, Satan."

Peter peeked under the tent and saw Goliath and the soldier in black. "I think you're right," he said. "Our problems might be even bigger than we thought."

The adventure bag shook under Peter's arm. He pulled out the scroll and unrolled it. Two words glowed and transformed into the words: BIGGER THAN. Peter read the scroll in a whisper, "FEAR _____. GOD IS BIGGER THAN

ANY PROBLEM." He quickly put the scroll away and peeked under the tent.

"You must destroy him!" said the soldier.

"Don't worry," said Goliath. "I will smash him like a little bug!" Goliath stomped his huge foot on the ground.

Peter felt the ground shake.

"Don't underestimate him," said the soldier in black. "Some people say he is the future king, and we can't miss this opportunity to destroy Israel and their future king." The soldier in

black leaned back and rubbed his chin. "I have a plan."

Goliath leaned forward. "What is your plan?"

"At first, I will protect you with my shield," said the Soldier of Darkness. "Then I will sneak around and attack him from behind! He'll never see it coming."

"That's cheating!" growled Goliath. "But I like it."

Peter grabbed Mary's arm and pulled. "We have to warn David."

Peter, Mary, and Hank headed back to the Israelite camp. They ran down into the valley and waded through the stream. Hank growled at something behind a big rock.

"Come here," said a voice from behind the rock. "Don't be afraid. It's me."

Peter looked. It was Michael the angel.

"Where have you been?" asked Mary.

"Why haven't you been helping us?" said Peter.

"God and I have been with you the whole time," said Michael. "I helped scare away the wolves. Peter, I held your feet when you leaned over the ledge to help David. I stood between Mary and the bear."

"I didn't see you," said Peter.

"You don't need to see to believe," said Michael.

"It's hard," said Peter.

"It can be," said Michael. "But you have to trust God. You also need to be on the lookout for the enemy, Satan. I've heard he is trying to stir up some trouble in the Philistine camp."

"I think we found him," said Mary. "We heard him planning a sneak-attack on David," said Mary.

"Yeah," said Peter, "and he was dressed all in black."

Michael crossed his arms. "That does sound like Satan," he said. "He can be very sneaky."

"Come on, Mary," said Peter. "We have to go and warn David!"

"You can't," said Michael.

"Why not?" asked Peter.

"Rule number three," said Michael. "It might change the future."

"Oh, that's right," said Mary. "We can't."

"David has his battle," said Michael. "Now you have yours."

"How can we battle Satan?" said Mary. "He has all that armor—and weapons."

"You have armor too," said Michael. "You have the armor of God." He held up his shield. "You have the shield of faith, the body armor of righteousness, the belt of truth, the shoes of peace, the helmet of salvation, and the sword of the Word of God."

Peter looked down and didn't see anything but a robe and his adventure bag. "I don't see any armor."

"Trust God," said Michael. "Stand your ground against Satan, and God will protect you." He spread his mighty wings. "And remember, you only have one day left to solve the secret of the scroll." He flew into the star-filled sky.

Peter, Mary, and Hank snuck back into the camp and went to sleep.

FACING THE GIANT

The battle horn blasted. Peter sat up and rubbed the sleep out of his eyes. He looked over and saw David on his knees with his hands lifted up to the sky.

"O Lord, you are my rock and my shield," David prayed. "Give me strength and rescue me from my enemy." Then he stood and picked up his staff. "I'm ready to face the giant."

Mary brushed sand off her robe. "We have a big day ahead of us."

Peter picked up the adventure bag. "We're ready too."

"Ruff!" Hank whined and licked David's hand.

"Don't worry, Hank. I'll be okay," said David.

They made their way across the hilltop and looked down into the valley. Peter turned toward the Israelites' camp. The soldiers were grabbing their swords and shields. They lined up behind David, who stared in silence into the valley.

Peter turned back. "Are you afraid?"

"Maybe a little," said David. "But I know God is with me and will help me."

"That's right," said Peter. "He always has and he always will."

The slow and steading pounding of the drums echoed across the valley.

The Philistines were preparing for battle too.

Peter watched as David descended into the valley with nothing but his staff in one hand and his sling in the other. David stopped at the small stream running through the valley and bent down. He picked five stones out of the stream and put them in his pouch.

The drumbeat grew louder and louder. The Philistine army lined up on the hill across the valley.

"Halt!" shouted the Philistine commander.

The Philistines pounded their spears on the ground. "Goliath! Goliath! Goliath!" they chanted.

Goliath marched to the front. The soldiers cheered for their champion. He looked down into the valley and laughed a grizzly laugh. He marched into the valley with his shield-bearer, the Soldier of Darkness, leading the way. Goliath stopped about twenty feet away from David.

Peter squinted. He could see Goliath's eyes narrowing. Peter thought he looked angry and offended.

"You come to fight me with a stick?" shouted Goliath. "Do you think I'm a little dog?"

"Ruff!" Hank barked. Now he was offended.

Goliath shook his massive spear. "I will destroy you," he snarled at David.

The Soldier of Darkness pounded the shield against the dusty ground.

"Come here!" Goliath yelled. "I will give your flesh to the birds and wild animals!"

David stood his ground. "You come to me with a sword and spear!" shouted David. "But I come to you in the name of the Lord of Heaven's army, the God of Israel."

Goliath shook with anger.

"Today, the Lord will defeat you!" said David.

Goliath raised his spear above his head.

David dropped his staff. He reached into his pouch, pulled out a stone, and put it in his sling. He ran straight at the giant swinging the sling round and round. Then he sent the stone flying through the air. It flew over the shield and hit Goliath right between his eyes.

Goliath wobbled and fell with a thud. A cloud of dust surrounded his motionless body.

Silence filled the valley. Then cheers rose from the Israelite army.

The Soldier of Darkness looked at the fallen giant. He dropped the shield and ran.

Peter pointed. "Look, he's coming around behind David, just like he said he would."

David didn't seem to notice the Soldier of Darkness—he was focused on the fallen giant. The Israelite soldiers didn't seem to notice either.

"What should we do?" asked Mary.

Peter's heart pounded in his chest. "We have to stop him! Let's go!"

No Time to Waste

Peter ran down into the valley as fast as his feet could carry him. He could hear Mary and Hank behind him.

Peter looked ahead. The Soldier of Darkness was sneaking up behind David. They had to hurry.

They ran past the Soldier of Darkness and stood between him and David.

"Well, look who it is!" snarled the Soldier of Darkness. "You three always seem to show up at just the wrong time!"

"Grrrr!" Hank growled.

"Get out of my way!" shouted the Soldier of Darkness.

"No!" said Peter. He didn't move. Neither did Mary or Hank.

The sound of the Israelites' cheers came across the valley. Peter looked over his shoulder and saw David holding up Goliath's sword in victory.

Peter turned back to the Soldier of Darkness. Anger filled the soldier's cold, dark eyes.

The Soldier of Darkness pulled out his long, silver sword. "That boy may have stopped my giant, but he won't stop me! I will destroy him!"

"We know your plan," said Peter. "And it's not going to work!"

The Soldier of Darkness pointed his sword at Peter. "Who's going to stop me?" he hissed. "You don't even have any weapons or armor."

Peter looked at the tip of the sharp sword. His heart pounded. Then he remembered Michael's words about the armor of God. "God will help us!" he shouted.

The Soldier of Darkness looked around and snickered. "I don't see God anywhere," he said. "It's just you and me." He took a step forward.

Peter remembered Michael's words about the shield of faith. "You don't have to see him. I believe in God!" he said. "And he is with us!"

Peter's faith was like a shield. It stopped the Soldier of Darkness in his tracks.

"God said David will be king!" said Mary. "And his word is always true."

These words of truth hit the Soldier of Darkness like a powerful sword. He stumbled back.

Peter looked up the hill and saw the Israelite soldiers charging down into the valley. Then he looked over his shoulder and saw the Philistine soldiers fleeing. David joined the Israelite soldiers as they chased the Philistine soldiers away.

Peter looked back at the Soldier of Darkness. "You will not win, Satan!"

Peter felt the bag shake by his side. He reached in and pulled out the scroll. Peter and Mary looked at the scroll. The final word glowed and transformed into the word: NOT.

Peter read the scroll: "FEAR NOT. GOD IS BIGGER THAN ANY PROBLEM!" He felt the ground shake. When he looked up, he saw the Soldier of Darkness staggering toward them holding the sword over his head.

"I will put an end to you meddling kids!"

shouted the Soldier
of Darkness.

Peter grabbed
Mary's hand and held
up the scroll. He
saw the sword
swinging toward
them. Then the
ground crumbled beneath their feet and they fell
safely into Great-Uncle Solomon's library.

Peter stood up and brushed himself off.

"That was too close," gasped Mary.

"*Woof!*"

The red wax seal transformed into a gold
medallion. Peter stared at the medallion. It had a
crown inscribed on it.

Great-Uncle Solomon burst through the door
carrying the harp. "You're back! Tell me about
your adventure!"

Peter told him about the sheep and the wolves. He told him about the Dark Valley of Death and how David taught him to overcome fear.

Mary told Great-Uncle Solomon about meeting David and his family. Then she told him about Goliath and the Soldier of Darkness.

"I hope David became king," said Peter.

Great-Uncle Solomon put down the harp and pulled his big, red Bible off the bookshelf to tell them the rest of the story. He told Peter and Mary how David became one of Israel's greatest kings. "He was also a great poet and musician," he said.

Mary picked up the harp and played a few notes.

Great-Uncle Solomon's eyes widened. "How did you learn to play?"

Mary strummed

the strings. "David taught me," she said. "And he taught me on *this* harp."

Great-Uncle Solomon jumped up. "I knew it!" he said. "I knew it was King David's harp!"

"Is there more to the story?" asked Peter.

Great-Uncle Solomon sat down and continued. "Oh yes," he said. "Even though David was a great king . . . another King was coming . . . and he would be the greatest King of all."

"Who?" asked Mary.

Great-Uncle Solomon set the Bible back on the shelf. "That is a story for another day."

Peter looked at the gold medallion in his hand. He couldn't wait to hear the lion's roar again.

Do you want to read more about the events in this story?

The people, places, and events in *The Shepherd's Stone* are drawn from the stories in the Bible. You can read more about them in the following passages in the Bible.

1 Samuel chapter 16 tells how David was chosen to be king.

Matthew 18:12–14 tells the parable of the Lost Sheep.

1 Samuel chapter 17 tells the story of David facing Goliath.

The Book of Psalms is filled with King David's poems and songs. You can find out how he overcame fear by reading: Psalm 23, Psalm 27:1, Psalm 34:4, Psalm 56:3–4, and Psalm 77:11.

CATCH ALL
PETER AND MARY'S
ADVENTURES!

In *The Beginning*, Peter, Mary, and Hank witness the Creation of the earth while battling a sneaky snake.

In *Race to the Ark*, the trio must rush to help Noah finish the ark before the coming flood.

In *The Great Escape*, Peter, Mary, and Hank journey to Egypt and see the devastation of the plagues.

In *Journey to Jericho*, the trio lands in Jericho as the Israelites prepare to enter the Promised Land.

In *The Shepherd's Stone*, Peter, Mary, and Hank accompany David as he prepares to fight Goliath.

In *The Lion's Roar*, the trio arrive in Babylon and uncover a plot to get Daniel thrown in the lions' den.

In *The King Is Born*, Peter, Mary, and Hank visit Bethlehem at the time of Jesus' birth.

ABOUT THE AUTHOR

 Mike Thomas grew up in Florida playing sports and riding his bike to the library and the arcade. He graduated from Liberty University, where he earned a bachelor's degree in Bible Studies.

When his son Peter was nine years old, Mike went searching for books that would teach Peter about the Bible in a fun and imaginative way. Finding none, he decided to write his own series. In The Secret of the Hidden Scrolls, Mike combines biblical accuracy with adventure, imagination, and characters who are dear to his heart. The main characters are named after Mike's son Peter, his niece Mary, and his dog, Hank.

Mike Thomas lives in Tennessee with his wife, Lori; two sons, Payton and Peter; and Hank.

For more information about the author and the series, visit www.secretofthehiddenscrolls.com.